The Life of Benjamin Franklin

Victor Greene

Infomax Readers

Rosen Classroom™

New York

Published in 2013 by The Rosen Publishing Group, Inc.
29 East 21st Street, New York, NY 10010

Book Design: Katelyn Londino

Photo Credits: Cover commons.wikimedia.org/wiki/File:Benjamin_Franklin_1767.jpg/Wikipedia.org; p. 4 commons.wikimedia.org/wiki/File:Benjamin_Franklin_by_Joseph-Siffred_Duplessis.jpg/Wikipedia.org; p. 5 Kean Collection/Staff/Archive Photos/Getty Images; p. 6 commons.wikimedia.org/wiki/File:Benjamin_Franklin_National_Memorial.jpg/Wikipedia.org; pp. 7, 23 (printer) commons.wikimedia.org/wiki/File:Franklin_the_printer.jpg/Wikipedia.org; pp. 8, 15, 23 (newspaper) iStockphoto/Thinkstock.com; p. 9 Comstock/Thinkstock.com; pp. 10, 23 (library) Charmaine A Harvey/Shutterstock.com; p. 11 Photo Researchers/Photo Researchers/Getty Images; pp. 12, 23 (glasses) © iStockphoto.com/NejroN; pp. 13, 23 (stove) commons.wikimedia.org/wiki/File:Franklin_stove.jpg/Wikipedia.org; p. 14 Leemage/Universal Images Group/Getty Images; p. 16 commons.wikimedia.org/wiki/File:Writing_the_Declaration_of_Independence_1776_cph.3g09904.jpg/Wikipedia.org; p. 17 Creatas/Thinkstock.com; p. 18 commons.wikimedia.org/wiki/File:Franklin%27s_return_to_Philadelphia_1785_cph.3g09906.jpg; p. 19 Herbert Orth/Contributor/TIME & LIFE Images/Getty Images; p. 20 commons.wikimedia.org/wiki/File:Houdon_-_Benjamin_Franklin_(1778).jpg/Wikipedia.org; p. 21 Photodisc/Thinkstock.com.

ISBN: 978-1-4488-8992-1
6-pack ISBN: 978-1-4488-8993-8

Manufactured in the United States of America

CPSIA Compliance Information: Batch #WS12RC: For further information contact Rosen Publishing, New York, New York at 1-800-237-9932.

Word Count: 189

Contents

Benjamin Franklin was
an important American.

Ben was born in 1706.

He came from a big family.

Ben did many things
to make America great.

Ben's first job was as a printer.

His brother was a printer, too.

Books cost a lot of money when Ben was alive.

Ben thought that people should be able to read books for free.

So, Ben set up one of America's first libraries.

Ben was an inventor, too.
An inventor makes or thinks
of something new.

One of Ben's inventions
was a special kind of eyeglasses.

He also made a new kind of stove.
It didn't use as much wood
as other stoves!

Ben was an inventor
so he could help people.

Ben also wrote letters
to help our country make laws.

The letters became laws in 1776.

These laws gave Americans freedom.

Freedom means that nobody can tell you how to live.

Ben also saw
many parts of the world.

He went to other countries
to talk about America.

Ben had a busy life.

He lived until he was 84.

Ben did a lot for our country.

We still honor him today!

Who Was Ben Franklin?

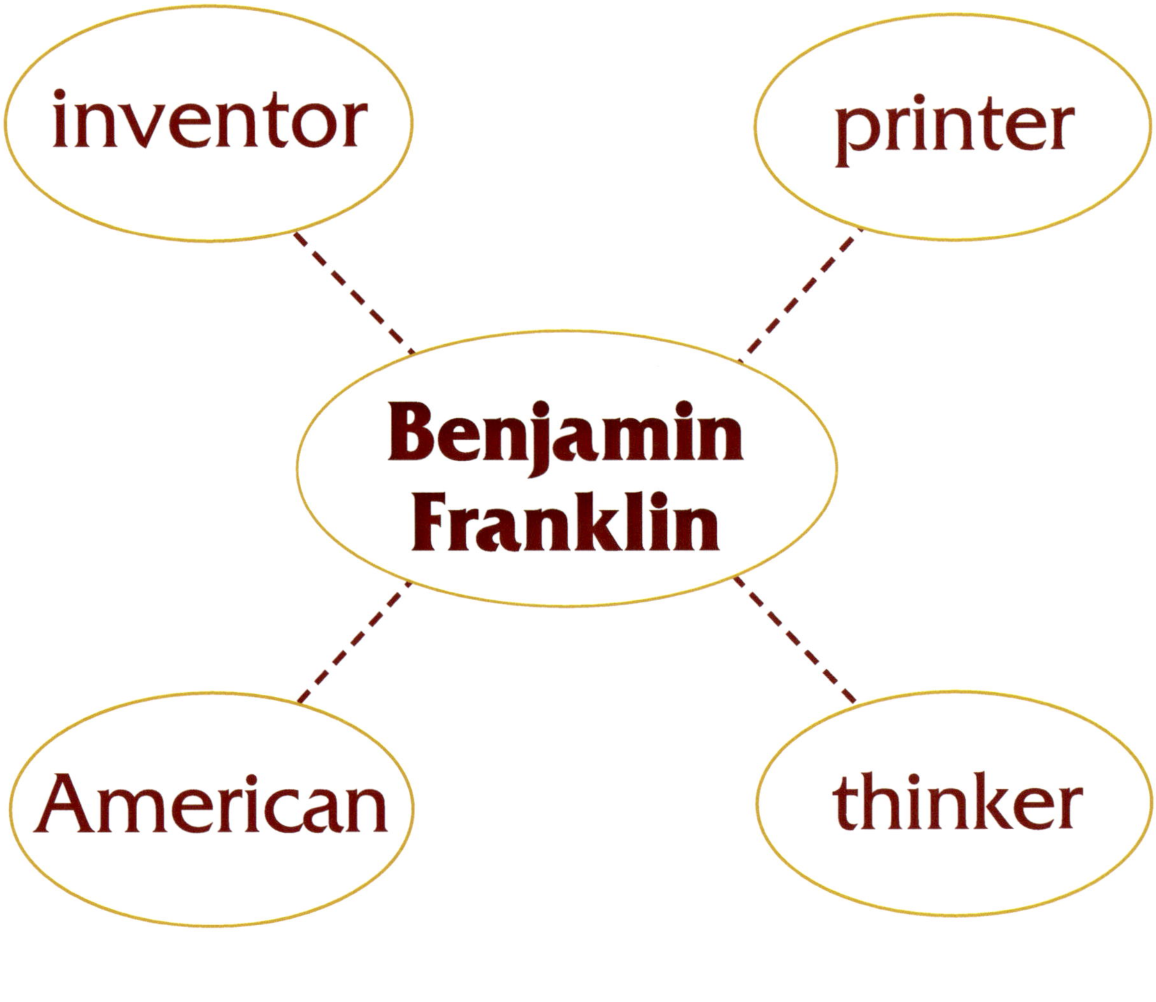

Words to Know

eyeglasses

library

printer

stove

Index